Juan Bobo
GOES TO WORK

A PUERTO RICAN FOLKTALE

RETOLD BY
**MARISA
MONTES**

ILLUSTRATED BY
**JOE
CEPEDA**

HarperCollinsPublishers

To my parents, Mary and Rubén Montes,
who taught me to be proud of my family and of my heritage.
And to my husband, David Plotkin,
for his constant support and never-ending belief in me.
—M.M.

For Dan, Sylvia, Elliott, Samantha, and Sara
—J.C.

ACKNOWLEDGMENT

Special thanks to my aunt, Ida Santiago, a delightful and beloved elementary-school teacher in Puerto Rico, for relentlessly searching out and sending me obscure volumes of Puerto Rican folklore. Thanks also to my aunt, Dr. Carmín Montes Cumming, for being my Spanish-language consultant and for always encouraging me to write. —M.M.

AUTHOR'S NOTE

For generations, Puerto Rican children have been entertained by the antics of the irrepressible Juan Bobo, who is the most popular hero of Puerto Rican folklore. *Bobo* means "simple" or "foolish." Juan Bobo, or "Simple John," is the Puerto Rican version of the town fool. He is the creation of the Puerto Rican country folk, or *jíbaros,* and arises from a mixture of the Spanish, African, and native Taino cultures. There are many stories about Juan Bobo; most of the classic tales depict rural Puerto Rico at the beginning of the twentieth century.

Because much of Puerto Rican folklore has its roots in European and African folklore, many Puerto Rican stories are similar to those in other cultures. The story of a foolish boy carrying the cheese on his head and pulling the ham on a string also appears in folktales of other countries. Different versions of this story exist even in Puerto Rican folklore. There are also several versions of the story of Juan Bobo going to work—the constant in each is that Juan Bobo can never get things right.

In addition to translating the story from the original Spanish and retelling it in my own style, I made a few minor changes. This is how folktales have evolved through the years: One storyteller adds a new twist, another storyteller embellishes a bit here, yet another embellishes there, and perhaps another, as I have done, changes the ending.

Juan Bobo Goes to Work
Text copyright © 2000 by Marisa Montes
Illustrations copyright © 2000 by Joe Cepeda

Printed in Hong Kong by South China Printing Company (1988) Ltd.

http://www.harperchildrens.com

Library of Congress Cataloging-in-Publication Data
Montes, Marisa (Marisa Isabel)
Juan Bobo goes to work: a Puerto Rican folktale / retold by Marisa Montes; illustrated by Joe Cepeda.
p. cm.
Summary: Although he tries to do exactly as his mother tells him, foolish Juan Bobo keeps getting things all wrong.
ISBN 0-688-16233-9 (trade)—ISBN 0-688-16234-7 (library)
1. Juan Bobo (Legendary character) Legends. [1. Juan Bobo (Legendary character) Legends.
2. Folklore—Puerto Rico.] I. Cepeda, Joe, ill. II. Title. PZ8.1.M765Ju 2000 398.2'097295'02—dc21 99–28799 CIP

1 2 3 4 5 6 7 8 9 10
❖
First Edition

In the highlands of Puerto Rico lived a silly peasant boy.
He was so silly he often got confused. Sometimes he got
things backwards. Other times he misunderstood things
completely. So everyone called him Juan Bobo, which
means "Simple John."

But Juan Bobo tried very, very hard to do things right.

One day his mother told him to go find work. Juan Bobo replied, "*Está bien*, Mamá. All right. Where should I look?"

"Ask the farmer for a job," said Doña Juana. "When he pays you, hold the money in your hand. Do not put it in your pocket."

Juan Bobo ran to the neighboring farm.

"*Buenos días,* Don Pepe. Good day," said Juan Bobo.
"*¿Me puede dar trabajo?*"

"You want a job?" Don Pepe looked Juan Bobo up and
down. He grunted. "You're pretty scrawny. What can you
do?"

"Anything, *señor.* I am a very good worker."

Don Pepe handed Juan Bobo a basket full of beans.

"Shell these *habichuelas.* Put the beans in the
wheelbarrow. Pile the shells on the ground."

Juan Bobo sang as he worked. He tossed the shells into the *carretilla*. And he piled the *habichuelas* on the ground. When he was done, Juan Bobo said, "Don Pepe, I finished my work."

The farmer stared at the shells in the wheelbarrow. "¡Qué bobo! What a foolish boy! What have you done with the beans?"

Juan Bobo's smile faded. "I thought you wanted the shells in the *carretilla* and the beans on the ground."

Don Pepe sighed. "It's all right, Juan Bobo. You have worked hard." He handed the boy a few coins. "Take this money to your mother."

Juan Bobo beamed. *"Muchas gracias, señor."*

On the road home Juan Bobo thought about his
mother's warning. "*¿Qué me dijo?* What did she say?"

Juan Bobo finally remembered. He put the coins in his
pocket and skipped home.

"Mamá! Here is the money I earned." Juan Bobo
reached inside his pockets. All he found were large holes.

"But Juan Bobo," said Doña Juana, "I told you to hold
the money in your hand. Your pockets have holes."

Juan Bobo hung his head.

"It's all right," she said with a sigh. "Take this burlap
bag. Tomorrow go back to the farm to look for more work.
When Don Pepe pays you, put the payment in the bag."

The next morning Juan Bobo set out early. Don Pepe had Juan Bobo milk one of his cows.

"First tie up *la vaca,*" said Don Pepe. "Then milk her and set *la leche* aside. When you are done, put the cow back in the stable."

Juan Bobo listened carefully. He did just as he was told.

First he tied the cow's front legs together. Next he tied her hind legs together. Then he milked her and set aside the milk.

Now it was time to return the cow to the stable.

Juan Bobo pulled the cow. Then he tugged. Then he yanked.

But the cow would not move.

Juan Bobo tried pushing the cow.

Still the cow would not budge.

"What is wrong, silly *vaca*? Have you turned to stone?"

Don Pepe saw what was happening. He cried, "Juan Bobo, the cow's legs are tied. She cannot walk like that!"

Juan Bobo laughed. "And I thought she had turned to stone."

Don Pepe removed the ropes and took the cow to the stable.

Then he handed Juan Bobo a pail of fresh milk. "Here, Juan Bobo. Take this milk to your mother in return for your work."

"Gracias, Don Pepe."

Juan Bobo poured
the milk into his burlap
bag and flung it over his
shoulder.

He set out for home. The
milk dripped from the bag
and down his back. By the
time he reached home, he
was drenched in milk.

"¡*Llueve leche,* Mamá! It's raining milk!"

Juan Bobo's mother shrieked. "Oh, Juan Bobo! You put the *leche* in the bag, and it leaked. Next time carry the pail of milk on your head."

"I will do just that, Mamá," said Juan Bobo. "*Así lo haré.*"

The next day Juan Bobo's mother told him to ask the grocer for work.

"And Juan Bobo, try not to lose your payment."

At the grocery store Juan Bobo asked Señor Domingo for a job.

"Can you sweep?" asked the grocer. *"¿Puedes barrer?"*
"Sí, señor. I am a very good sweeper."
Señor Domingo handed Juan Bobo *una escoba,* a broom. When Juan Bobo finished sweeping, the store gleamed.

The grocer was pleased. "Such a good job deserves a large reward. Take this cheese to your mamá as payment for a job well done."

"*Muchas gracias, señor.*" Juan Bobo happily took the large hunk of *queso.*

On the way home he remembered what his mother had told him about the milk pail. Juan Bobo took off his straw *pava*.

He put the cheese on his head.

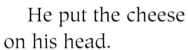

But the noonday sun was very hot. Before long the cheese began to melt. It dripped down his face.

"Mamá! Mamá!" he cried, running home. "¡*Llueve queso!* It's raining cheese!"

Doña Juana placed her hands on her head. "Ay, Juan! What will I do with you?"

Juan Bobo hung his head. "*Lo siento*, Mamá. . . . I'm sorry."

The next week Doña Juana told Juan Bobo to return to the grocer. "This time take some string. Tie up whatever the grocer gives you."

Señor Domingo had been very pleased with Juan Bobo's last job. So he again had Juan Bobo sweep the store. When Juan Bobo finished, the floor shone brightly.

The grocer clapped Juan Bobo on the back. "Wonderful job, Juan Bobo. Today I will pay you with my largest *jamón*. You deserve a big ham."

The boy took the heavy ham in his arms and set off for home. Soon his arms grew tired. He remembered what his mother had told him.

"I must tie it up with the string." Juan Bobo tied the string around the ham and dragged the ham behind him.

"Mamá is a very smart woman. It is much easier to pull a huge *jamón* than to carry it."

Juan Bobo passed the house of a very rich man. On the balcony a beautiful girl sat in a rocking chair.

Everyone in the *barrio* knew her sad story. The girl was very ill, *muy enferma*. Many doctors had examined her. Each one agreed that if the girl did not laugh soon, she would die.

When Juan Bobo passed by, the girl looked up. He skipped toward her, dragging the huge ham behind him. Nibbling the ham was every cat and dog in the neighborhood.

The girl laughed and laughed and laughed—*se rió y se rió y se rió.*

The rich man heard his daughter's laughter and ran to the balcony. He saw what was making her laugh.

"*¡Ven acá, muchacho!*" he called to Juan Bobo. "Come here, boy! You have saved my daughter's life!"

"I'm sorry, *señor,*" said Juan Bobo. "I must hurry home to Mamá!"

Juan Bobo reached home, leading a parade of cats and dogs. But the ham had disappeared.

That night Juan Bobo and Doña Juana did not feast on hearty baked ham. Instead, they had a meager meal of *arroz y habichuelas*, rice and beans.

But the rich man never forgot what Juan Bobo had
done. Every Sunday he made sure that Juan Bobo
and his mother had a plump, tender ham
on the table.

GLOSSARY

arroz (ah-RROS) rice

arroz y habichuelas (ah-RROS ee ah-vee-CHOOEH-lahs) a Puerto Rican dish made of white rice topped with a thick bean sauce

Así lo haré (ah-SEE loh ah-REH) That is how I'll do it.

barrer (bah-RRER) to sweep

barrio (BAH-ree-oh) neighborhood

bobo (BOH-boh) fool; simpleton

buenos días (BOOEH-nos DEE-ahs) good day

carretilla (kah-rreh-TEE-yah) wheelbarrow

enferma (en-FER-mah) sick, ill

escoba (es-KOH-vah) broom

está bien (es-TAH beeyen) all right; it is all right; fine

gracias (GRA-seeyahs) thank you

habichuelas (ah-vee-CHOOEH-lahs) beans, such as kidney beans

jamón (hah-MON) ham

jíbaros (HEE-bah-rohs) Puerto Rican country folk

leche (LEH-cheh) milk

Lo siento (loh SEEYEN-toh) I'm sorry.

Llueve (YOOEH-veh) It's raining.

¡Llueve leche! (YOOEH-veh LEH-cheh) It's raining milk!

¡Llueve queso! (YOOEH-veh KEH-soh) It's raining cheese!

¿Me puede dar trabajo? (meh POOEH-deh dar trah-BAH-hoh) Can you give me a job?

muchacho (moo-CHA-choh) boy

Muchas gracias (MOO-chas GRA-seeyahs) Thank you very much.

muy enferma (mooee en-FER-mah) very sick

pava (PAH-bah) straw hat

¿Puedes barrer? (POOEH-des bah-RRER) Can you sweep?

¡Qué bobo! (KEH BOH-boh) What a fool!

¿Qué me dijo? (KEH meh DEE-hoh) What did she/he (or you—formal) tell me?

queso (KEH-soh) cheese

rió/ se rió (rree-OH; seh rree-OH) laughed; she/he (or you—formal) laughed

señor (seh-NYOR) Mister, Mr.; owner or master

sí (SEE) yes

trabajo (trah-BAH-hoh) a job

vaca (BAH-kah) cow

¡Ven acá, muchacho! (ben ah-KAH, moo-CHA-choh) Come here, boy!